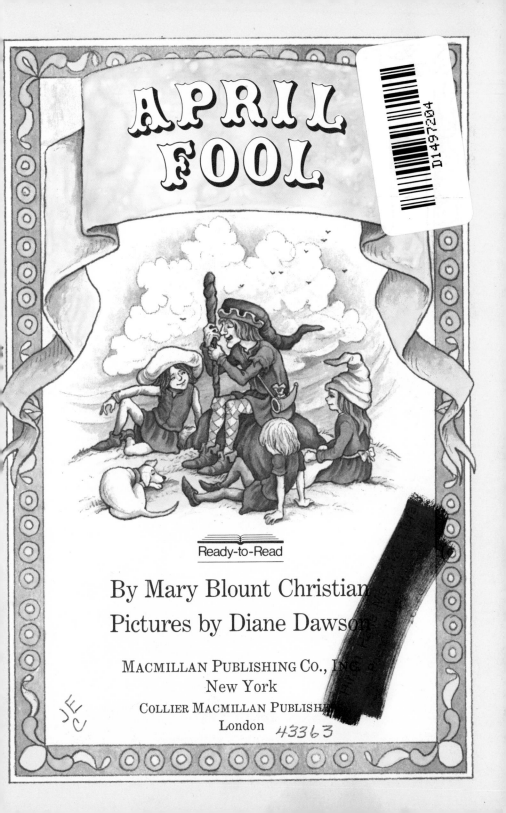

APRIL FOOL

Ready-to-Read

By Mary Blount Christian

Pictures by Diane Dawson

MACMILLAN PUBLISHING CO., INC.
New York
COLLIER MACMILLAN PUBLISHERS
London

43363

Macmillan Publishing Co., Inc., 866 Third Avenue, New York, N.Y. 10022. Collier Macmillan Canada, Inc. Printed in the United States of America. *Library of Congress Cataloging in Publication Data.* Christian, Mary Blount. April fool. (Ready-to-read) *Summary:* The clever people of Gotham keep the king from building a hunting lodge outside their village by convincing him that they are fools. [1. Folklore—England] I. Dawson, Diane. II. Title. III. Series. PZ8.1.C4628Ap 398.2'1'0941 [E] 81-3782 ISBN 0-02-718280-0 AACR2 10 9 8 7 6 5 4 3 2 1

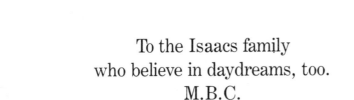

To the Isaacs family
who believe in daydreams, too.
M.B.C.

To Nonee and Daddle with love.
D.D.

Seth liked to daydream.
He told his dreams
to the village children.
The other grownups called him
Seth the Dreamer.
They said he did
nothing useful.

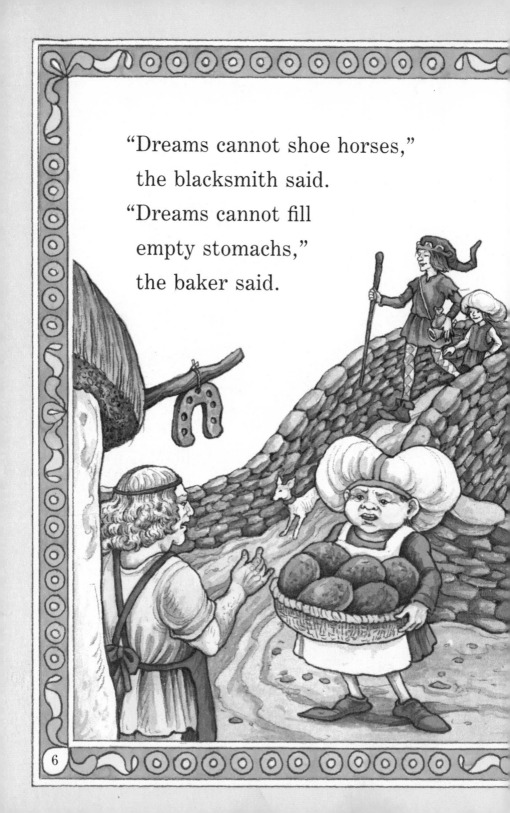

"Dreams cannot shoe horses,"
the blacksmith said.
"Dreams cannot fill
empty stomachs,"
the baker said.

"Dreams cannot light
the darkness,"
the candlemaker said.
"Dreams cannot make money,"
the tax collector said.
Seth the Dreamer just smiled.

It was the last day of March.
Seth sat telling a dream
to the children.
Suddenly he stopped.
He saw a horse
on the far-off hill.
Strangers were coming.
One rider held the king's flag.
The villagers were excited.
They had never seen
King John before.

King John stopped to rest.
The flag man rode up
to meet the people.
"The king will look around
your town tomorrow," he said.

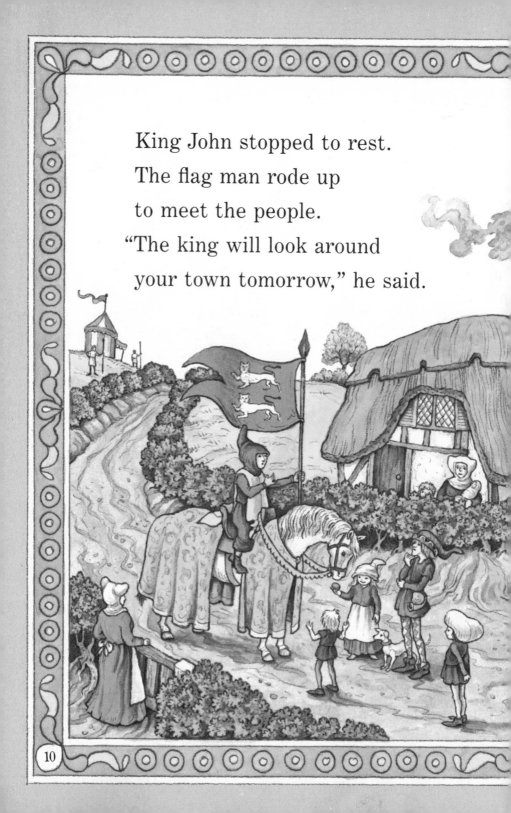

"If he likes what he sees
he will build a house here.
He will come to hunt and fish
all the time.
This is an honor
for your town," he said.
Then he rode off.

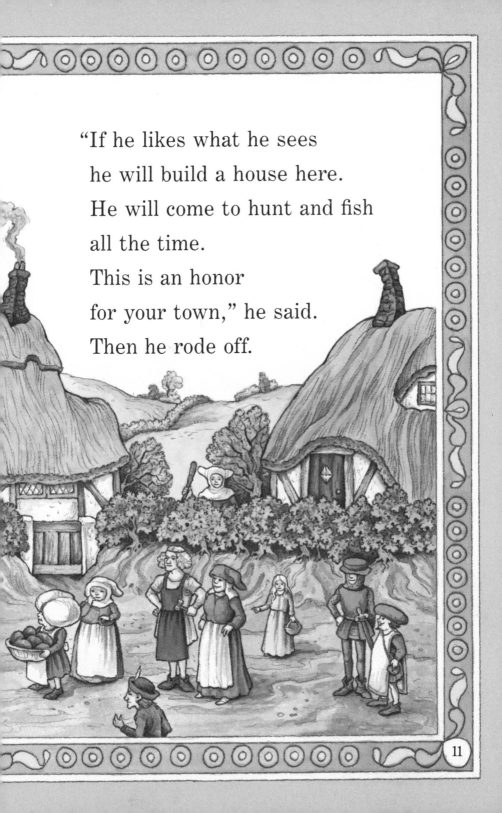

The farmer said,
"Some honor!
King John visited
my brother's town once.
Now it is part of
the king's highway.
It is crowded
with noisy strangers.
There are too many horses.
It is not safe
to cross the street.
You can be robbed
or run over."

Seth nodded.

"Where the king rides,
the land becomes public road.
King John will take
whatever land he wants."

"This is terrible,"
the tax collector said.

"Public roads mean travelers.
That means more work for me."

"Thieves follow travelers,"
the sheriff of Gotham said.
"The town will not be
safe and peaceful any more."
The game warden said,
"Who would dare catch
a bigger fish than the king?
We will have to settle
for only the smallest ones."

"If the king stays here
so will his horses,"
the blacksmith said.
"I will not have time to shoe
our own horses any more."
"And I will be busy
baking *his* bread,"
the baker said.
"You will have to bake
your own bread if he stays here."

"And make your own candles,"
the candlemaker said.
"You will grow your own grain, too,"
said the farmer.
"The king will take
most of *my* grain."
"What about our children?"
the baker's wife asked.
"Our sons will join his army."
"Our daughters will marry
his soldiers," said the
blacksmith's wife.
"All our children will be gone!"
the game warden's wife cried.

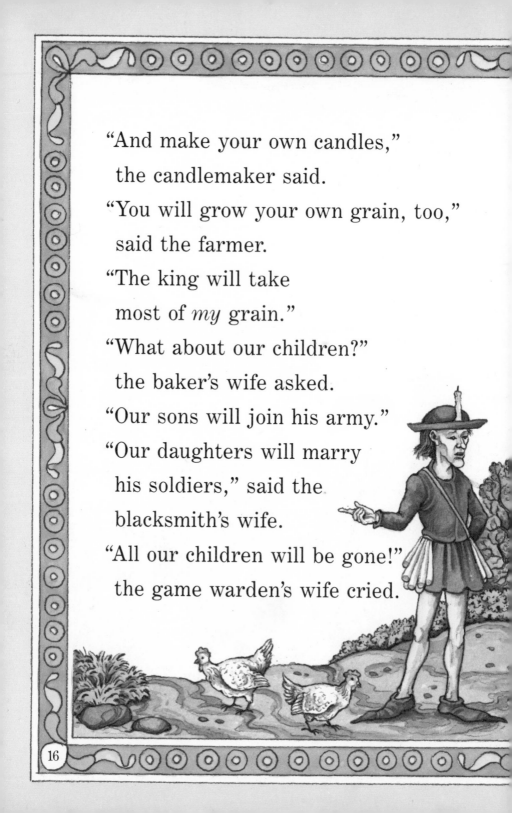

"Let's run!" the baker said.
"Let's fight!"
the blacksmith said.
"Let's not let him in!"
the farmer said.

"King John has a terrible temper,"
said Seth.
"He might cut off your heads.
Which of you will dare
to tell the king
he cannot come here?"
Seth asked.
"Look," he said,
"the king is already angry."
He pointed to where
the king was camped.
The king was having
a temper tantrum.

He kicked the flag man.
He stomped the ground.
He shouted and waved
his fists in the air.
Then he kicked his tent
until it fell apart.

The farmer moaned.
"The blacksmith is right.
We must fight for our lives!"
The blacksmith cried,
"The baker is right.
Run!"
Seth raised his hand.
"Wait!" he cried.
"Maybe there is a way
we can save our town
and our heads, too."

"But how can we do that?"
the blacksmith asked.
Seth the Dreamer just smiled.
"Maybe I can dream up a way,"
he said.

On the first day of April,
King John rode into Gotham.
No one came out to greet him.
No one cheered for him.
The king was angry.
His face grew red.
Then the king rode by a farm.
His anger turned to surprise.

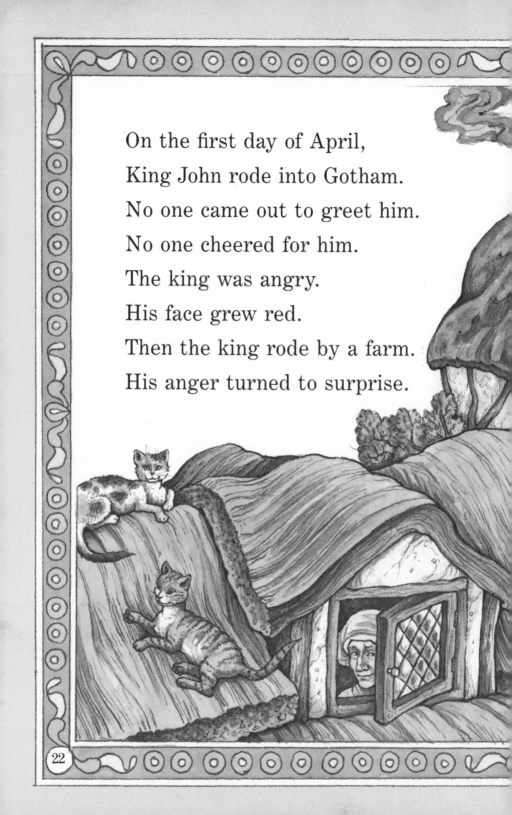

The farmer struggled to pull
his plough through the field.
His ox walked behind the plough.
"What a fool!" the king said.
"The *ox* should pull.
You should walk behind."

The farmer bowed.

He hid his smile from the king.

"Why, that is so much easier!"
he said.

"How clever you are, King John."

The king rode past the river.
The game warden carried
a bucket of fish.
One by one he threw them
into the river.
"I am drowning the stupid things,"
he said to the king.
"They won't play games with me."

"What a fool!" the king said.

"Fish cannot play games.

And they do not drown, either."

The game warden bowed his thanks.

The king rode on.

He came to the bakery.
The baker and the candlemaker
stood on the roof.
The sheriff stood on the ground.
They pulled and tugged
and pushed on a mule.
They tried to get the mule
up on the roof.

The mule brayed and kicked
and would not budge at all.
"Why are you trying to get
the mule on the roof?"
the king asked the baker.
The baker bowed.
"The roof leaks, sire.
We must patch the holes."
"But what does that have to do
with the mule?" the king asked.
The sheriff raised an eyebrow.
"The mule is carrying
all our tools, sire.
What good are tools to us
if they are not on the roof?"

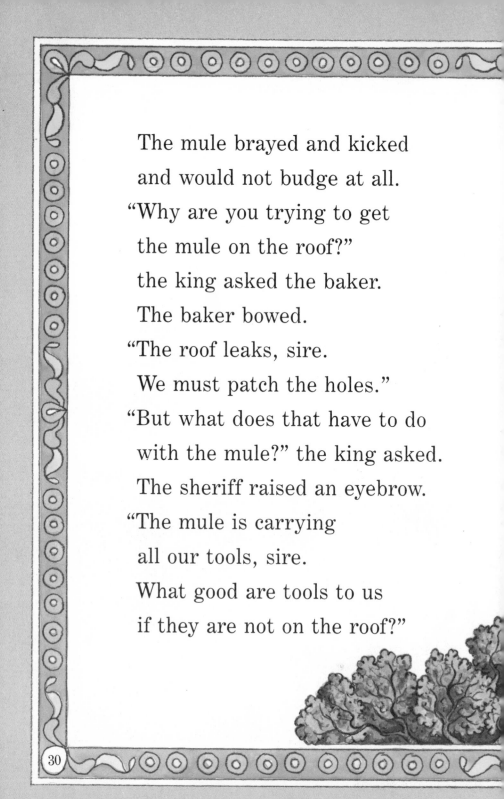

"What fools you are!"
the king cried.
"The mule has more sense
than you do."
He rode on.

The baker's wife and her son
sat in the garden.
The baker's wife picked a flower
and gave it to her son.
Her son tore off the petals
and put the stem in a vase.

The king rode past
the blacksmith's wife.
She screamed and cried
and pounded the highchair.
Her daughter fed her whey.

The king rode past
the game warden's wife.
She fried eggs in their shells.
"Are they *all* fools?"
the king said.
"Does anyone in Gotham
have good sense?"

"We have good sense,"
Seth said to the king.
He pulled up a bucket of water
from the well.
The tax collector looked
at the bucket and nodded.
Then Seth threw the water back
into the well.
"What are *you* doing that
makes good sense?" asked the king.
"We want to see if we can pull up
the same water more than once,"
Seth said.
"You are fools, too!"
the king yelled.

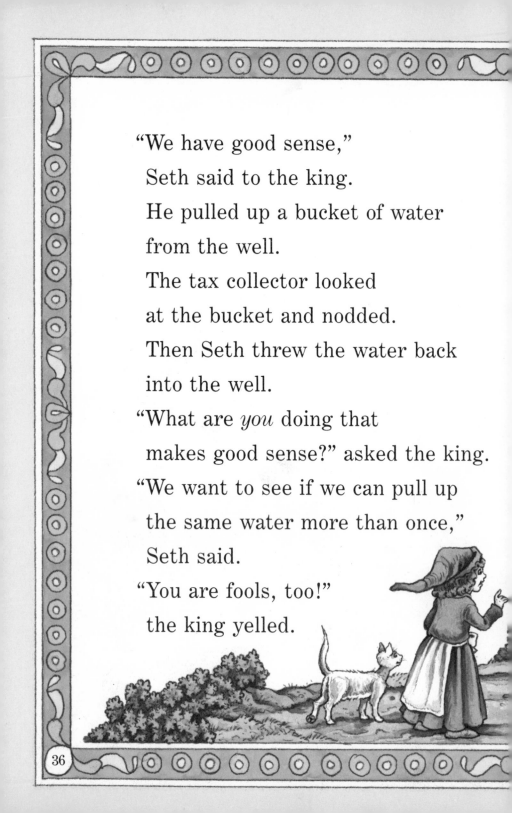

"How can you know
the water is the same?"
"That is easy," Seth said.
"See here? We marked
the first bucket with an X.
And we have pulled it up
every time."

The king rode on
to the blacksmith's shop.
The blacksmith greeted him.
"Shoe your horse, kind king?"
"At last!" King John cried.
"Someone who is not a fool!"
The blacksmith brought out
four pretty little slippers.
"These shoes will look
very nice on your horse,"
the blacksmith said.
"Fools!" the king yelled.
"You are *all* fools."

The king rode back
to his soldiers.
"I cannot cut off
the people's heads
just because they are fools,"
he said.
"But I do not want
to live with them."
The king and his men left
to find another town.

The blacksmith went back
to shoeing his horses.
The baker went back
to baking his bread.

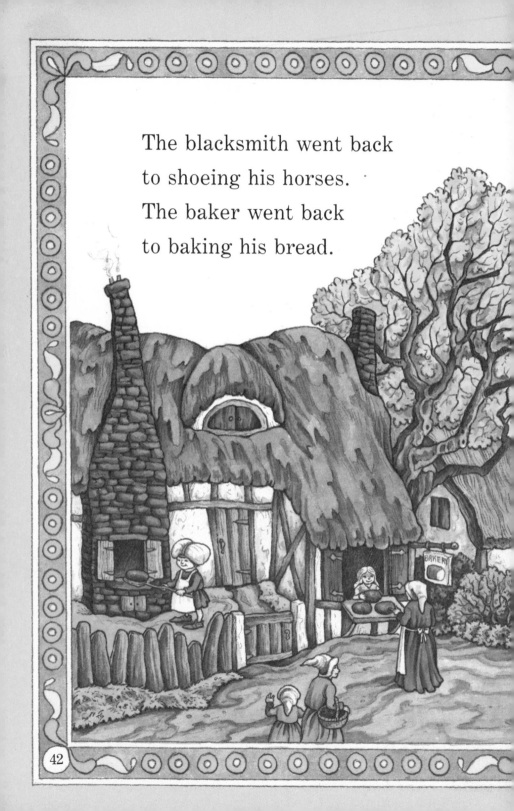

The farmer went back
to planting his corn.
The tax collector went back
to counting his money.

The baker's wife went back
to digging in her garden.
The blacksmith's wife went back
to feeding her child.
Everything was the same
as it had been before
the king came.

Except sometimes
everyone stopped work.
They sat with the children
and Seth the Dreamer.
"Tell us again,"
they begged him.
"Tell us how you dreamed up
the first April Fools."

AUTHOR'S NOTE: During the reign of King John in the thirteenth century, it was English law that any land traveled by the king immediately became public roads, and the king was free to seize whatever land pleased him for his own use. According to the legend, the people of Gotham, near Nottingham, kept King John from building a hunting lodge near their village and turning their quiet little back roads into much-traveled public roads. They knew the king would punish them for their little rebellion unless they had a good excuse. And the only excuse forgivable was if he thought they hadn't the sense to know better. From that time on, Gotham had the reputation of being a village of fools, and to accuse anyone of being from Gotham was to call him silly. But it is said that King John really did throw just such a temper tantrum as described here. Perhaps it happened just this way and perhaps it did not. But some say this may have been the beginning of our own April Fools' Day.